My First Time

Written by

Ken Davenport

and

People Just Like You

Inspired from the website
www.MyFirstTime.com
created by Peter Foldy & Craig Stuart

SAMUEL FRENCH

FOUNDED 1830

NEW YORK HOLLYWOOD LONDON TORONTO

SAMUELFRENCH.COM

ISBN 978-0-573-66382-6   Printed in U.S.A.   #15763

IMPORTANT BILLING AND CREDIT
REQUIREMENTS

All producers of *MY FIRST TIME must* give credit to the Author of the Play in all programs distributed in connection with performances of the Play, and in all instances in which the title of the Play appears for the purposes of advertising, publicizing or otherwise exploiting the Play and/or a production. The name of the Author *must* appear on a separate line on which no other name appears, immediately following the title and *must* appear in size of type not less than fifty percent of the size of the title type.

Written by (50%)
Ken Davenport
and
Real People Just Like You

Inspired from the website www.MyFirstTime.com (25%)
created by Peter Foldy & Craig Stuart

Original Off-Broadway production directed and produced by
Ken Davenport

No other credit other than the title shall be the larger than the credit afforded the Authors.

In addition, the following credit must be listed at the bottom of the title page in a reasonably sized type:

For more information on MY FIRST TIME
visit www.MyFirstTimeThePlay.com

MY FIRST TIME is a BestOfOffBroadway.com production

Slide images referenced in the script are available from
Samuel French, Inc. for licensed productions.
Please email info@samuelfrench.com for more information.

MY FIRST TIME, directed and produced by Ken Davenport, officially opened Off-Broadway at New World Stages in New York City on July 28, 2007. The original cast was as follows:

MAN #1	Bill Dawes
MAN #2	Josh Heine
WOMAN #1	Cydnee Welburn
WOMAN #2	Kathy Searle

US for MAN #1	Dana Watkins
US for MAN #2	Marcel Simoneau
US for WOMAN #1	Natalie Knepp

A NOTE FROM THE AUTHOR

My First Time is about one of the few things that almost every single person on this planet has in common. It doesn't matter if you live in New York or New Delhi, if you're Bill Clinton or Bill Gates, more than likely at some point in your life, you are going to have sex for the first time.

But if so many of us go through it, how come we don't talk about it?

That's exactly why I created *My First Time*, to get people talking about this ultimate rite of passage that so many of us expect to be perfect, but most likely was anything but!

My First Time has great opportunities for its actors to create wonderful characterizations of very unique people. It is the director's responsibilities to encourage them to create distinct and unique individuals of varying ages, dialects, societal classes, etc., while at the same time making sure that these characterizations do not at all become caricatures or cartoons. The strength of *My First Time* is in the fact that the stories are real, and therefore its characters and the people that speak these stories must also be "real."

The physical production should be kept very simple, in order to allow the stories to be the spotlight. The laptop in the opening scene, the stools, and the projection screen and its corresponding slides are all that are required. Anything more might detract from the sincerity of the play.

The costumes should be simple as well, with nothing that causes one actor to stand out more than another. Try and implement a small splash of a unique color on each actor.

We encourage the use of small props, etc., that may help an actor define his/her character (e.g. glasses, a bible), etc. Once again, the secret is subtlety. Make sure you do not use too many items that detract from the strength of the words themselves.

The most unique quality of the play is the survey cards and how they are interpolated into the play. Should you have any questions about the process, please don't hesitate to email info@myfirsttimetheplay.com, and we will talk you through it.

Lastly, actual first times are rarely as fun as they should be. Let your audience know that it's ok to have fun. Let them know it's ok to laugh at their own first times. As the last slide says, "Maybe then we can concentrate on what's really important: The Next Time."

PRESHOW

(PRESHOW MUSIC, DEALING WITH THE SUB-JECT OF SEX AND/OR FIRST TIMES, BEGINS.)

(A blue card is on each audience member's seat, asking the following questions:

1. Are you male or female?

2. Are you a virgin? If your answer to this question was "No," continue to question #3? If your answer was "Yes," you have completed the survey.

3. How old were you when you lost your virginity?

4. Where were you when you lost your virginity?

5. What was your partner's name?

6. Do you still keep in touch with him/her?

7. Did you feel pressured to lose your virginity?

8. Did you plan your First Time in advance?

9. Did you use contraception?

10. How would you describe your first time: INCRED-IBLE, GOOD, NOT GOOD, AWFUL

11. If your first sexual partner was here right now, what would you say to him/her?

(The surveys are collected throughout the pre-show by ushers and brought backstage.)

(A crew member inputs the data from the cards into a spreadsheet in order to tabulate the statistics required in the slides later on in the show.)

(Another crew members sorts through the cards and finds the 16 "best" names, ages, locations and com-ments, transferring those to other cards for use in the

show.) (**NOTE:** *You do not have to take an entire audience member's card. Often the "best" locations aren't the "best" comments, so mix and match so that the final comments represent your strongest audience responses for all categories.)*

(A white laptop is center stage on a stand and in its own light.)

(Four white stools are upstage in a row, also glowing in their own light.)

(Each stool has a white pocket on the top created with a piece of white card stock, where the actors store their survey cards when not in use.)

(Behind the stools is a projection screen which displays the following slides throughout the preshow:

PRESHOW SLIDES #1-40: [AUTO REPEAT]

#1. Stemming from the greek word for Virgin, parthenos, a parthenologist is a person who specializes in the study of virgins and virginity.

#2. "I lost my virginity when I was 14. And I haven't been able to find it."

– David Duchovny

#3. "Virginity can be lost by a thought."

– St. Jerome

#4. "I think I was 16. It was on a baseball diamond at about 11 p.m. in Canton, Ohio in the fall. I had gotten drunk on some stolen Jim Beam from my grandmother that I smuggled into my Kiss thermos. And it lasted about 35 seconds. It was pretty shameful and just something that I had to get out of the way."

– Marilyn Manson

#5. "It was also on the kibbutz that I first had intercourse. It was a beautiful and romantic experience. We walked hand in hand under the starry sky to a barn on the kibbutz where hay was stored and climbed up a ladder to the second story. One thing I'm not happy about is the way we dealt with the issue of contraception. I know much, much better now, but in those days I thought hoping was enough."

– Dr. Ruth

#6. "Men see women as sex objects when women act like unpaid whores. Now it is difficult to find the male who values virginity, purity and innocence when females dress like babes and perform oral sex and intercourse without even having to be fed dinner."

– Dr. Laura

#7. "I don't know which story was my first: Was it the back of the car or my uncle's alley? All I know is I was 15, and it did not live up to its expectations."

– Playboy Playmate Jenny McCarthy

#8. Since its inception, there have been over 36 million visits to MyFirstTime.Com, accounting for over 7 million hours, or 800 years.

#9. "My first time was horrible. It was just nasty. Me and my cousin had these two chicks who were sisters, and we took them into a stairwell in the projects. I could never get comfortable. There wasn't enough space and I couldn't get anything right. You have to be comfortable for your first time."

– Rapper Ja Rule

#10. From Dictionary.com:

"Virgin [vur-jin]– noun

   1. a person how has never had sexual intercourse.

2. An unmarried girl or woman

3. Ecclesiastical. An unmarried, religious woman, esp. a saint.

4. The Virgin, Mary, The Mother of Christ.

5. Informal. Any person who is uninitiated, uninformed, or the like: He's still a virgin as far as hard work is concerned."

#11. From UrbanDictionary.com:

"Virgin [vur-jin] noun

1. Person who has not yet had sex. Largely believed to be mythological.

2. A person who has not yet engaged in sex because they are waiting for true love.

3. A person who has not yet engaged in sex because they are so socially crippled that whenever they are around the opposite sex they begin to hiss and fart uncontrollably.

4. In North Carolina, any girl who can outrun her brothers.

5. Without alcohol."

#12. "Abstinence for me is about romance. It has nothing to do with my relationship with God. It's definitely a bonus in that department, but it's nothing spiritual. It's about giving something special to that person you're going to spend the rest of your life with."

– Jessica Simpson

#13. Would you want a cell phone to go off during your First Time?

#14. Neither would we!

#15. Please silence your phones, or put them on you know what.

#16. Approximately 75% of all the visitors to

MyFirstTime.com are from the U.S. The remaining 25% are from around the globe.

#17. "I'm proud to say that I am a virgin, and I don't hide the strength God has given me. You have to learn to respect yourself before you can start respecting other people."

– LA Lakers Forward and NBA All-Star, A.C. Greene, who later married his wife at the age of 38, still a virgin.

#18. For her 17th wedding anniversary, Jeanette Yarborough wanted to do something special for her husband. In addition to planning a hotel getaway for the weekend, Yarborough paid a surgeon $5,000 to reattach her hymen, making her appear to be a virgin again.

#19. "It's the ultimate gift for the man who has everything," says Yarborough, 40 years old, a medical assistant from San Antonio.

– Revirgination.net

#20. "I always thought of losing my virginity as a career move."

– Madonna

#21. On MyFirstTime.Com, the average user spends an average of 12 minutes and 17 seconds.

#22. On CNN.com, the average user spends an average of 8 minutes and 30 seconds.

#23. "I want you to listen to me. I'm going to say this again. I did not have sexual relations with that woman."

– Bill Clinton

#24. 77% of teens classify oral sex as sex.

#25. Rosie Reid sold her virginity in an auction on the internet to avoid graduating from university with debts of $36,700. The 'lucky winner' was a BT engineer, she claims. She sold her virginity for $20,500.

#26. "Sex within marriage is the only kind that's truly fun and exciting – the kind that lasts for a lifetime. I'm glad I waited."

– Kirk Cameron

#27. Every day, approximately 12,000 people visit the website MyFirstTime.Com.

#28. "It is one of the superstitions of the human mind to have imagined that virginity could be a virtue."

– Voltaire

#29. Teens with a Catholic parent 72% are more likely to not have had sex because they are worried what their parents will think than those with a Protestant parent 63% or another religious background 57%.

#30. "Virginity is a bubble in the froth of life – one prick and it's gone."

– Anonymous

#31. "It is difficult to believe in a religion that places such a high premium on chastity and virginity."

– Madonna

#32. More Americans lose their virginity in June than in any other month. Prom is also in June. Coincidence?

#33. Your old virginity is like one of our French withered pears: it looks ill, it eats dryly."

– Shakespeare

#34. "The world has suffered more from the ravages

of ill-advised marriages than from virginity."

– Ambrose Bierce

#35. "Losing your faith is a lot like losing your virginity. You don't realize how irritating it is until it's gone."

– Anonymous

#36. Those who make a public pledge to abstain until marriage delay sex, have fewer sex partners and get married earlier.

#37. There are men in Guam whose job is to travel the countryside and deflower young virgins, who pay them for the privilege of having sex for the 1st time.

#38. Over 38,000 stories have been submitted to MyFirstTime.Com

#39. The word "farm" appears 174 times in those stories.

#40. The word "cousin" appears 610 times.

SLIDE #40 FADES TO BLACK [AUTO]

(END OF PRESHOW SLIDE PRESENTATION)

PROLOGUE

(The following Show Slides [#2-6] should start only after the change from Preshow Slides to the Show Slides, but with at least one minute remaining in the second to last preshow song:

SLIDE #2:

Every day, sexual intercourse takes place 120 million times on earth.

SLIDE #3: AUTO

According to population statistics, this means that 1 out of every 25 people have had or will have sex today.

SLIDE #4: AUTO

There are_____ *(insert number of people)* in this audience.

SLIDE #5: AUTO

Will the _____ *(insert number of people)* that have had sex or will have sex today please raise their hands.

SLIDE #6: AUTO

Will the other _____ *(insert number of people)* please applaud for the lucky _____ *(insert number of people from Slide 5)*.

SLIDE #6 FADES TO BLACK AUTO.

(House lights fade to half. Lights on stools and labtop brighten.)

(Final preshow song begins to play.)

SLIDE #7-11:

There is/are _____ *(insert number of people)* virgins in this audience.

(This Slide stays up for the entire last song, but the number of virgins should increase through the song, e.g. "1...3....5," until....)

(Preshow music fades out.)

(House lights go to black as...)

SLIDE #11 FADES TO BLACK.

(Crew removes laptop and table from stage.)

(Cast enters Stage Right. All sit on stools except MAN #1 who stands downstage. From stage right to stage left, the order is MAN #1, WOMAN #1, MAN #2, WOMAN #2.)

(voiceover begins)

PETER FOLDY. *(voiceover)* Hello. My name is Peter Foldy. In 1996 my buddy Craig and I started a website called MyFirstTime.com. I can't mention Craig's last name because he still hasn't told his mom about it. A lot of people asked us why we did it, and the truth is we wanted to know if everyone else's first time sucked as bad as ours did. Since then, over 40,000 true stories from all over the world have been submitted to the site by people just like you. And now, for the "First Time," those words will be spoken. So sit back and listen close. One of these stories might be yours.

SLIDE #12: [WITH TYPING SOUND]

Story #26999

Where It Happened:

My Room

(lights up)

(MAN #2, WOMAN #1 & WOMAN #2 look at MAN #1, who begins to speak.)

MAN #1. Well friends...I'm sitting here wrapped in a towel at my computer and my girlfriend is lying naked in my bed. We were virgins until tonight. She e-mailed me earlier and told me about this website. She said she would come over later after I had a chance to read some of the stuff on it. I read the stories for two hours straight until she snuck in. She sat down next to me and she said, "Wouldn't it be cool if we could write our story here?"

SLIDE #12 FADES

(**MAN #1** *sits down.*)

Scene I

MAN #2. To start off, this is my story. Not some story I made up for fun.

WOMAN #1. I never thought I would write about my sex life and especially about my first time.

WOMAN #2. First of all, I'm not a slut.

MAN #1. This story is absolutely true...even though her name has been changed.

WOMAN #1. I want to tell my story because it seems so different from the kinds I've been reading here.

MAN #2. I needed to tell someone about this as I can't tell my best friend.

WOMAN #2. I guess looking back on the whole thing after all these years, I can be a bit more analytical about it.

MAN #1. I remember my first sexual experience. I was alone at the time.

MAN #2. Some people might be offended by my first time.

WOMAN #1. I lost my hymen in a bicycle accident.

WOMAN #2. I have kept this secret long enough.

MAN #1. I owe it all to my Mom.

(All look at **MAN #1.***)*

MAN #2. While you are categorizing first time stories, file mine under "clumsy and awkward!"

WOMAN #1. My first experiences were about as significant as taking Mom's car up and down the driveway when nobody was looking.

MAN #1. I know you aren't supposed to have a physical relationship with your step-sister...

(All look at **MAN #1.***)*

WOMAN #2. I had two First Times. Really.

MAN #2. I got laid on Saturday, May 12, 1990 at 7:15 PM.

WOMAN #1. I was deflowered on Valentine's Day.

MAN #1. 1937, a depression year.

WOMAN #2. Early this morning.

MAN #2. It would be the first time for us both.

WOMAN #1. I come from a family who believes in arranged marriages and that's how it happened. On my wedding night in the summer of 1951.

WOMAN #2. Our first time was the day before the prom and we screwed ourselves silly until it was time to leave for college.

MAN #1. My first time was with a lady that I did odd jobs for. The last time I cut her lawn, she invited me in for iced tea. She said she was grateful for all the things I'd done for her and that a woman has a special way to express her gratitude: if I came into her bedroom, she would give me a proper goodbye present.

WOMAN #1. I had known him for several years. We went to the same gymnastics gym in Missouri. I remember watching him do his routines. He had the most incredible iron cross.

WOMAN #2. This guy was everything I dreamed of. He read Sartre, Tolstoy, and rode a motorcycle.

MAN #2. We met at bible camp.

WOMAN #1. I grew up down the street from Dave. We pulled each others pants down and watched each other pee in the bathroom.

MAN #1. Now slut is a pretty harsh word, but it was no secret that she put out for 50 bucks. One night I asked her if she would do it for 25.

MAN #2. I was in a high school presentation of *Peter Pan.* I had a part as one of the pirates. The Indians were all girls. They were dressed fairly risque, for 1978 small town Canada. They wore a two-piece bikini made out of rabbit fur. I'd have to close my pirate's frock to hide the hard-ons they used to give me.

WOMAN #2. We worked together on the Clinton campaign.

MAN #1. We both worked for Pizza Hut.

WOMAN #1. I worked as a lifeguard at a local indoor pool. My duties included closing the pool down at 9:00 p.m. Pete would usually arrive a half-hour before close and give me a good reason to kick everyone out a little early. After that, we'd lock all the doors and swim together. One night after the pool closed, Pete was late so it gave me time to shower, perfume, and slip into a pair of very sexy panties. He arrived with a nice bottle of plum wine. My favorite. I told him that tonight was the night.

MAN #2. She was the type of girl that made guys heads turn when she came walking by.

WOMAN #2. He was cute as hell with shaggy blond streaked hair and smooth tanned skin.

MAN #1. She had on white bell bottom corduroys and a black t-shirt that said "future fox."

WOMAN #1. He was handsome, but I did not think I should be friends with him because his tribe and my tribe have been enemies for hundreds of years.

MAN #2. If you took softballs, sliced off about a third and glued them to your chest, you have a fair approximation of her shape and size.

MAN #1. I couldn't keep my eyes off her.

WOMAN #1. I couldn't get him off my mind.

MAN #2. I was mesmerized by her boobies.

WOMAN #2. He looked like Matthew Broderick from *Ferris Bueller's Day Off.*

WOMAN #1. He reminded me of Harrison Ford.

MAN #1. A miniature Pamela Anderson.

WOMAN #2. He was an absolute hunk.

WOMAN #1. He was an asshole.

MAN #2. She had a real nice ass.

WOMAN #1. He was so beautiful.

WOMAN #2. He was so hot.

WOMAN #1. He was so…

WOMAN #2. …married.

MAN #2. And God fearing.

WOMAN #1. His name was John.

MAN #1. There was this guy at camp called Kyle.

WOMAN #2. Darren had an identical twin.

WOMAN #1. Un des marins, Patrick, m'aborda en anglais.

MAN #1. Vivo con mi hermana Maria Luisa.

WOMAN #2. Kevin was in my chemistry lab. One Friday night in November I went back to his dorm room. He put on a Boz Skaggs disk. He got my shirt off by putting marbles down it.

MAN #2. Teresa was a Hispanic girl and would have been quite attractive if not wearing old, baggy clothes with her hair all stringy and her face grimy.

MAN #1. Someday I'll tell my Dad about Liz, but not until the statute of limitations has run out.

WOMAN #1. Rob got this book called Kama Sutra.

MAN #2. She was from Florida and her name was Cheri, but she pronounced it "Cherry."

MAN #1. Whenever she wears her hair in a page-boy style, she looks a lot like Marcie, of the Peanuts cartoon. She has a fantastic memory, and is just as smart as the cartoon Marcie. So although her real name is the sweetest sound I will ever know, I'll call her Marcie.

WOMAN #2. His name was Chase.

MAN #1. Elaina.

WOMAN #1. Shawn.

MAN #2. Claire.

WOMAN #2. Moose.

MAN #1. Mrs. Gavaghan.

WOMAN #1. Sven.

MAN #2. Carmen.

WOMAN #2. Rob.

MAN #1. Mrs. Gavaghan.

WOMAN #1. Rick.

WOMAN #2. Rick.

MAN #2. Rick.

WOMAN #1. Tony Goat Boy.

MAN #1. Kitty.

WOMAN #2. Ken The Cocksucker.

WOMAN #1. Mr. X.

MAN #2. Elise isn't her name, but let's protect the guilty.

(A CREW MEMBER comes onstage and hands MAN #1 four packs of four survey cards. MAN #1 takes a pack of cards and passes the rest down. The others do the same, taking one pack and passing the remaining down. They read from the survey cards. Names listed below are examples; names during the following section should be what is on the actor's actual survey cards:)

MAN #1. *(reading)* Julie.

WOMAN #1. *(reading)* Joseph.

MAN #2. *(reading)* Erin.

WOMAN #2. *(reading)* Eric.

MAN #1. *(reading)* Ashley.

WOMAN #1. *(reading)* Asshole.

MAN #2. *(reading)* Carol.

WOMAN #2. *(reading)* Robbie.

MAN #1. *(reading)* Don't remember.

WOMAN #1. *(reading)* Fred.

MAN #2. *(reading)* Andrea.

WOMAN #2. *(reading)* Christopher.

MAN #1. *(reading)* Linda.

WOMAN #1. *(reading)* Dwayne.

(MAN #2 puts down his cards.)

MAN #2. I didn't learn the woman's name. I didn't even get a good look at her face.

SLIDE #13:

Story #1851

Where It Happened:

At Convention

(MAN #2 steps downstage. ALL look at MAN #2.)

MAN #2. *(cont.)* I had a fight with my girlfriend. In an effort to cheer me up, my father, Karl, took me to his annual convention. I didn't see any wives there and the entertainment reflected it. There were some business meetings but we didn't attend. The last night I begged off claiming a headache. I was in a sound sleep when a naked woman climbed into bed with me. I was aroused before I fully came to. She threw a leg over me and inserted me. I thought I was in a wet dream initially. The cigarettes on her breath…I did what I was supposed to do mostly to get it over with. I wish I had thrown her out but I didn't. The pain was compounded by Karl having a woman of his own in the other bed. I noticed a condom on the floor beside Karl's bed but my woman didn't use one. Karl's answer was that my woman didn't need one since this was my first time. He was never "Dad" after that, but "Karl." I have since forgiven myself as there is only so much you can ask of a 15 year-old boy.

(Lights fade to black as….)

SLIDE #13 FADES to BLACK

*(*MAN #2 *sits.)*

Scene II

SLIDE #14: [AUTO]

In France, the average age of a person's first sexual experience is 16.8.

SLIDE #15: [AUTO]

In China, the average age is 18.2.

SLIDE #16: [AUTO]

In The United States *(or insert your country here),* the average age of a person's first sexual experience is...

SLIDE #16 FADES [AUTO]

(lights up)

WOMAN #1. You know what they say...that most people lose their virginity between ages 14 and 16? Well, I fall under that category as well. The story goes something like this...

(WOMAN #2 *steps downstage.)*

SLIDE #17:

Story #16264

Where It Happened:

My Friend's House

WOMAN #2. Evelyn and I had been friends forever. We were freshman and got picked on a lot. This guy in gym class had said something rude about Evelyn's breasts. She was really upset. That weekend I decided to cheer her up so I stayed at her house. Her mom made us dinner, we watched HBO, and decided to go to bed. We started talking about guys, but then I brought up the guy in gym. He *was* kinda cute after all, and she started to cry. I told her I was sorry. She turned the light out and we started to fall asleep. Her bed is really small so we were pretty close. When I stretched, my knee accidentally grazed her crotch. She made this funny sound. I whispered, "Sorry," but she sighed like she was disappointed. I could hear her breathing kinda heavy, so I got the nerve up and moved my hand onto her leg. She gasped, and I almost moved away before she made a sound of pleasure, and relaxed. Slowly I moved my hand down and under her gown. "Yes," she whispered. Evelyn took one hand and stuck it under my shirt. I'd never been so exited in my life! She climbed on top of me and we started kissing. Evelyn stopped and looked at me. "I love this," she said. All I could think to say was, "Yeah!" I felt stupid, but she smiled. She pulled the covers off and moved down to pull my panties off. As Evelyn kneeled down I thought I was going to explode. I almost wondered if she had done this before because she was incredibly good at it. I was trying to keep quiet but it was hard not to gasp or move. The bed was squeaky so I tried to stop but I couldn't. I was having my first orgasm and I didn't care if I was too loud! But now that I think about it her dad probably heard me. Evelyn looked at me and smiled, "Did you like that?" It was such a stupid question, so I didn't answer it…I just grabbed her. After, we put our clothes back on and laid in her bed. We didn't say a single word the rest of the night, it was too awkward, but I couldn't help throwing an arm and a leg over her, so we fell asleep holding each other. It wasn't the last time we did it, in fact, we're roommates now at the University of Ohio. She has a boyfriend and I still like to date, but Evelyn is my best friend, and she was my first time and it felt perfect. The end.

SLIDE #17 FADES.

(WOMAN #2 *sits.*)

MAN #2. My first sexual experience occurred at age 13. My partner was 28.

WOMAN #1. In eighth grade, I began to hear about a secret club.

MAN #1. In the morning she found out how old I was and went into a panic. I assured her I would never tell.

MAN #2. I don't know how old she was, because I was taught it was rude to ask a woman her age.

WOMAN #2. I did not have my cherry popped until September 15, 1984, 12 days before my 20th birthday. My friends had been fucking like rabbits since we were 13. I held out. Not because I was saintly or moral. I was afraid of the damn thing! Anything that could grow six inches and get that hard in a matter of seconds had to be dangerous.

WOMAN #1. I must have been the oldest virgin on earth before my first time.

MAN #1. 19 years old and a virgin. Now that's something you don't want to get around to the rest of your ship-mates.

MAN #2. I finished high school at 16, college at 20 and a masters in computer science by 22. So, here I am, 22 years old, making an ungodly amount of money and still a virgin.

WOMAN #2. I was getting real anxious about being a virgin.

WOMAN #1. I was going crazy.

MAN #2. I felt suicidal.

MAN #1. I was satisfied with masturbating.

(All look at MAN #1.*)*

I discovered that if I put two pillows in a plastic bag and put oil or lotion between them, I could fuck my pillows.

WOMAN #1. I had been masturbating since age 11.

MAN #2. I was masturbating furiously three or four times a day.

WOMAN #2. When I was 19, it just wasn't enough any more.

MAN #1. It was time I grew up and became a man.

WOMAN #1. It felt like every single person I knew had already had sex. I felt so naive. Something inside me was telling me it was time to find out what the big deal was.

SLIDE #18

Story #1853

Where It Happened:

Radio Station

(MAN #1 steps downstage and puts on a pair of glasses.)

MAN #1. In my freshman year of college, before the revolution of the sixties, I was teamed up with a girl for the midnight to two AM shift at the college radio station. I held the FCC license to supervise the transmitter, and she played records. Hormones finally wielded their power and we began carrying on. My first time was on Valentine's Day, 1962, a little after two AM. I showed up to our shift, kissed her and gave her a card. After the last techie left, I bolted the front door. I proceeded to remove my sweetie's blouse and bra while she was holding a conversation on the air. There was nothing she could do. I then hung a solid gold heart on a chain around her neck and sat down to the other mike to continue the show. I took off all my clothes. It was the first time I ever got naked in front of a girl though the bottom half of me was behind the console. The electricity between us made us both silly. Callers were asking what was with us. When we were accused of drinking, we recited Peter Piper picked a peck of pickled peppers. The show signed off and I read the FCC required announcement and played the National Anthem. As soon as I killed the transmitter she was all over me. She announced she had her own Valentine surprise. She said she would always treasure her gold heart and would I like to give her a memory to go with it. You bet I would. We made love for the three hours the station was off the air. It is a memory of a lifetime for me.

SLIDE #18 FADES TO BLACK.

(MAN #1 sits.)

(WOMAN #1 *steps downstage.*)

SLIDE #19 [AUTO]

Story #548

Where It Happened:

Luxury Hotel

WOMAN #1. All I thought about was parties and beer. When I pulled a D in algebra, my dad laid down the law. If I was not serious about school, I shouldn't look to him for money for college. He did offer to get me a tutor and one of my teachers recommended Matt, the class brain. Matt had to use a wheelchair on account of his cerebral palsy and was pretty much ignored by his class-mates...and me. But he was an excellent teacher. He made math actually interesting! Two nights before the SATs, I kissed Matt and asked him if he was interested in me. He said he thought I was the most beautiful girl in school and that he realized he didn't have any future with me as he was in a wheelchair. I felt so bad for him because he was really a nice guy and he treated me far more decently than my so-called boyfriends. I rubbed him through his trousers and he wasn't get-ting stiff and I asked if he was really interested in me. He started to cry and he told me that he couldn't get erections but that what I was doing felt awfully good. He asked me to lay on top of him. He kissed me and held me and told me that I was the first girl who did anything with him. The next Friday Matt took me to an expensive restaurant. It had a ladies menu with-out prices and Matt ordered in French. He asked if I would like to "go somewhere." I said I would be hon-ored. He had a room already rented at a "love motel." There was champagne in an ice bucket and a circular bed and a jacuzzi right in the bedroom. He lit some candles and turned off the lights and undressed me very slowly. I got in the jacuzzi. He got undressed, took off his leg braces and climbed in with me. We fooled around and explored each other. After a long while, he asked if I wanted to go all the way. I was not sure what he meant as he hadn't gotten an erection at all, but I was delighted to do anything he had in mind. With just the fooling around, it was absolutely the best sex I ever had. He had me move the candles over to the bed and he asked me to look away. Matt was injecting his penis with a hypodermic. In about ten minutes he invited me to put a condom on. The next morning Matt explained that he had to push his dad and the urologist to get the injection. It was embarrassing but it was one more lesson in taking charge of his life. Matt said that while he can't stand on his feet, he can stand up for himself. For any of you in high school: Take notice of any tigers in wheelchairs. He or she might be the ticket to a happy life.

SLIDE #19 FADES TO BLACK.

WOMAN #1 *sits.*

WOMAN #2. I lost my virginity when I was 14.

MAN #2. I was 17 years old at the time.

WOMAN #1. Sweet 16.

WOMAN #2. Staci and I were both 15. The two guys were both 18.

MAN #1. They looked 17.

MAN #2. 15 years old.

WOMAN #2. I was 14.

WOMAN #1. 13.

MAN #1. 12.

SLIDE #20

Story #20126

Where It Happened:

N/A

MAN #2. 34. *(beat)* And I'm still a virgin. I have the same urges as any guy, but I've waited this long and I want my first time to be with that very special woman I have yet to meet. I am sometimes embarrassed when I let men or women know that I've never had sex. I get a variety of reactions from very positive to very negative. Some women want to "help me out." But, I want my first time to be about more than sex. It isn't easy being a 34 year-old virgin. But I am confident that when I meet that special lady the wait will be worth it and the moment will be magic.

SLIDE #20 FADES TO BLACK.

WOMAN #2. I had just turned 21.

MAN #1. She had just turned 16.

WOMAN #1. He was going to be 18 in June.

MAN #2. I told her I was 16.

WOMAN #2. I said 14 almost 15 which I was to be in a month.

MAN #1. We were almost 18 years old.

WOMAN #1. Almost 14.

MAN #2. About 17.

WOMAN #2. Old enough.

(Cast prep cards.)

SLIDE #21

Story #20153

Where It Happened: N/A

WOMAN #1. I am responding to #20126, the 34 year-old virgin. You sound like a really great guy. I am a 42 year-old virgin and feel the same way you do about sex. It's sad, most men won't date women who will not engage in intercourse. I hope you stand by your feelings and meet that special lady soon. Society is cruel to us virgins, but we must not submit to their pressures. Good luck. I'm sure when you meet that special lady you will be a most kind, gentle and sensitive lover.

SLIDE #21 FADES TO BLACK.

(All read ages from cards. The following lines will various depending on the ages on the cards:)

MAN #1. *(reading)* 16

WOMAN #1. *(reading)* 15

MAN #2. *(reading)* 21

WOMAN #2. *(reading)* 14

MAN #1. *(reading)* 15

WOMAN #1. *(reading)* 15

MAN #2. *(reading)* 17

WOMAN #2. *(reading)* 22

MAN #1. *(reading)* 16

WOMAN #1. *(reading)* 17

MAN #2. *(reading)* 15

WOMAN #2. *(reading)* 15

MAN #1. *(reading)* 21

WOMAN #1. *(reading)* 14

MAN #2. *(reading)* 23

(**WOMAN #2** *steps forward.*)

SLIDE #22:

Story #34130

Where It Happened:

Older Sister's House

WOMAN #2. Yeah I know, 20 years old seems like an old age for a girl living in the 20th century to lose her virginity. I felt the same way. I was tired of not knowing what sex felt like or being able to talk about doing it when the topic came up. The truth is I waited so long because I wanted to be in love with the person, but I figured I better settle for lust. His name was Gary and we used to be boyfriend and girlfriend but he was too imma-ture. We stayed friends and would hook up all the time. One day I called him and said "Let's just have sex." We both lived at home so we made plans to meet at my sisters house. In minutes we were kissing like mad. Then I said, "Ok, Gary, let's not put this off any longer." I got on top of Gary and he slid in. We went really slow. I cried a little and said "ouch" a lot. He said he didn't want to hurt me and he wanted to stop but I said, "No!" After like 2 seconds he came and I was left unsastisfied and with a pain between my legs. So that's that.

(She starts to return to her seat and then changes her mind, turns and continues:)

As far as regrets I am glad I did it. I wasn't expecting the sex to be great, I just wanted to know how it felt.

(Blackout)

SLIDE #22 FADES TO BLACK.

(WOMAN #2 *sits in blackout.)*

SLIDE #23: [AUTO]

In the United States, *(or insert your country here),* the average age is...15.8 *(or insert your country's age here.)*

SLIDE #24: [AUTO]

In this audience, the average age of a person's first sexual experience is...*(insert audience statistic here)*

(lights up)

(WOMAN #1 *is faced upstage reading the final slide. She turns and looks at the audience with disapproval. She has a ribbon or barrette in her hair, making her look very prim and proper.)*

SLIDE #25: [AUTO]

Story #7690

Where It Happened:

N/A

WOMAN #1. I'm not trying to pass judgement on anyone. I just felt the need to say something to the guys that I'm hoping are out there that are virgins. I've noticed some entries from college-aged guys that write, often with a tone of embarrassment or regret, that they haven't had sex yet. They seem to wonder if there's something wrong with themselves. But as a 19 year-old college student, I want to say that there is nothing wrong with it, and you have no reason to be ashamed. Let's face it: it's easy to have sex. No matter what, I'm sure any guy could find some "slut" or prostitute that would sleep with him. So even if you don't consider yourself to be a virgin "by choice," in some ways you are, and that's something to be proud of.

MAN #1. Yeah...right.

(blackout)

SLIDE #25 FADES TO BLACK.

(**WOMAN #1** *sits in blackout.*)

Scene III

SLIDE #26: [AUTO]

An excerpt about planning your First Time from:

"The First Sexual Experience Guide"

on

www.sexual-health-resource.org

SLIDE #27: [AUTO]

"It is very important that the First Time someone has sex, everything should be done to make it a satisfying and exciting experience…

SLIDE #28: [AUTO]

…allow lots of time to have sex the first time…like a whole weekend…

SLIDE #29: [AUTO]

…avoid eating a heavy meal as this can make you sleepy…

SLIDE #30: [AUTO]

…you might like to bring along your favorite pillow."

– www.Sexual-Health-Resource.org

SLIDE #31: [AUTO]

_____% *(insert number from audience survey)* of the people in this audience planned their First Time.

SLIDE #32: [AUTO]

Story #1332

Where It Happened:

Her Parents' House

(lights up)

MAN #2. My birthday is on the 21st of December, and at 2 AM, my girl came into my room with coffee and cookies. She announced she had something serious to discuss. She said that I was the first person she had been intimate with. When I pointed out we hadn't been that intimate, she answered...

WOMAN #1. Exactly. I have been on the pill for a month now. I'm doing it for you and this is no small thing for me. My parents are OK about this, I'm OK with this, the question is are you OK with this?

SLIDE #32 FADES TO BLACK

MAN #1. We decided to do it on Valentine's Day.

WOMAN #1. Planning the deed was wonderful!

MAN #2. We would meet after work.

WOMAN #2. Look, I want to lose my virginity but I don't want to get treated too roughly. You are the *two* nicest guys I know.

WOMAN #1. I wore a simple white dress.

MAN #2. I wore a pair of soccer shorts, sandals, and shades.

WOMAN #2. I knew exactly how I wanted it all to be and planned the details carefully.

MAN #1. What happened this night was unplanned...but it couldn't have been more perfect.

SLIDE #33

Story #35373

Where It Happened:

His Home

(MAN #2 steps downstage.)

MAN #2. I was on the bus from school and a guy sitting next to me was listening to some pretty cool music. I started a conversation with him about it and he introduced himself as Sean. He said that he had all the band's CDs at his house if I wanted to borrow them. He lived pretty close to me so I walked back to his place. He then told me straight out he was gay, but I didn't have any problem with it. I just asked him what it was like, but nothing he said really shocked me. He came over and sat next to me. He asked me if I liked him and I said that he was quite good looking and very funny. He leaned forward and kissed me...on my lips! I was stunned for a bit then I gave him a little smile and leaned over...and kissed him back! We kissed for a while before he suggested we have a shower. I was really curious by now so we got undressed in front of each other. I got the biggest boner straight away. It was poking him but he just laughed. I asked him if I could have a close look at his body. He asked me to soap him all over, so starting from the top and moving down I slowly rubbed his chest and arms, before giving him a light back massage. It was then he suggested I finish the massage in the bedroom...

SLIDE #33 FADES TO BLACK.

(WOMAN #1 steps downstage.)

WOMAN #1. My first times were in the basement of my boyfriend Doug's house.

(WOMAN #2 steps downstage.)

WOMAN #2. I fixed up a love nest in an abandoned cabin in the reservoir woods. I cleaned it up, nailed plywood over the windows, put a lock on the door and furnished it.

(MAN #1 steps downstage.)

MAN #1. It was a typical 70's scenario...blacklight posters on the wall, the odor of marijuana in the air, and Led Zeppelin playing in the background.

WOMAN #1. His bedspread had NFL logos all over it. He had posters of Michael Jordan, Ken Griffey, Jr. and *Star Wars.* He also had Sports Illustrated Swimsuit pictures tacked up on the wall. I doubt he ever thought he would have the real thing on his bed.

WOMAN #2. We rented a suite at the Howard Johnson hotel, with a king-sized bed and everything!

MAN #2. We took a blanket out on the golf course.

MAN #1. We were on the subway in Washington, D.C.

*(As **MAN #1** speaks, the others relax into casual subway positions..)*

SLIDE #34:

Story #451

Where It Happened:

Subway

MAN #1 *(cont.)* It was jam packed, morning rush hour, I was going to Union Station. She was in a white T-shirt and cotton shorts that hung loose. She *(indicates* WOMAN **#1***)* kept watching me watch her. Each stop, as more people got on, we kept moving closer. The rocking of the subway and people pushing me caused my...to keep bumping her thigh, *(he almost 'bumps'* WOMAN **#1***)* and at the next stop, she shifted so that her butt was next to my.... I don't think she meant to do this and we were weren't really touching, but she smiled at me and I went ape. She smiled at me and I went ape. As the subway pulled out of the station, I bumped up to her. She looked back at me, smiled again, then looked off as if nothing was going on. Next thing I knew we were at Union Station. I moved to get off the subway. She moved in front of me to an open seat, yet still standing, she brushed her leg between mine and lifted her thigh against my...I got off the train and looked back at her. She smiled again and said...

WOMAN #1. Have a nice day.

MAN #1. Sex can't be better than that moment.

SLIDE #34 FADES.

WOMAN #2. We were like rabbits after that. Having sex in my bathroom. On the floor. Wherever there was the urge, we merged!

MAN #1. A basketball court.

WOMAN #1. In a graveyard.

MAN #2. Yellowstone National Park.

WOMAN #2. A carnival.

MAN #1. Church steps.

WOMAN #1. A cricket pavilion.

MAN #2. The Point.

WOMAN #2. Burger King bathroom.

MAN #1. A campsite somewhere in Pennsylvania.

WOMAN #1. Disneyland.

MAN #2. Bangkok.

WOMAN #2. In the middle of the "wave pool" at the local water park.

MAN #1. A janitor's room across from the Governor's office.

WOMAN #1. His dream was to lose his virginity on the football field.

MAN #2. Where else?

WOMAN #2. In his car.

MAN #1. Dans la voiture.

WOMAN #1. Mom's minivan.

MAN #2. A Geo Metro.

WOMAN #2. Back seat of my pinto.

MAN #1. A yellow Plymouth Roadrunner.

WOMAN #1. His super sweet 1978 black Ford F150.

(All but **WOMAN #2** *sit.)*

SLIDE #35:

Story #1058

Where It Happened:

In a Car

WOMAN #2. I had a brother four years younger. He was diagnosed with leukemia and eventually underwent a bone marrow transplant. It was an eight hour drive to the medical center so my parents lowered the back seats of the station wagon and placed a wide mattress for Luke and me to lie on because Luke was not so strong for such a long ride. Luke and I were curled up together under several blankets. Luke confided in me that he never had a relationship that had gone beyond kissing and he was afraid of dying a virgin. I continued to hold Luke in my arms as I came to a decision. When we stopped for McDonalds, I asked that Luke and I be allowed to sit at a table apart and my parents agreed. Luke and I had a discussion of what sex meant in our lives. I wanted Luke to understand that I was making a one time, lifetime exception for him, because it would be very wrong in ordinary circumstances. He made his objections about respect, incest, pregnancy. He was willing to refuse me. I put it to him that if he made the utmost effort to live, I would pay a small enough price if this would motivate him. He accepted. I went to the restroom and removed my bra and panties. I stocked up on paper towels. Most important of all I prayed. We all got into the car for the five hour leg of my trip. I removed my jeans. I lowered his jeans to his knees. We made no motion under the blankets. After a few minutes, I felt Luke's whole body convulse and he let out an almost inaudible short moan and a exhalation. My parents heard it and asked what was going on in back. I said that Luke was sleeping restlessly and must have been dreaming. We got our clothes organized and had twenty minutes of snuggling before the gas station. Luke's transplant took but he did not survive the infections while his immune system was shut down. We were never really privately alone again. That is my story. I have no interest in approval.

(**WOMAN #2** *looks at the audience for a beat then turns and sits.*)

SLIDE #35 FADES.

(*Cast reads audience members' location from cards.*)

MAN #1. *(reading)* Behind a Wal-Mart.

WOMAN #1. *(reading)* High School bathroom.

MAN #2. *(reading)* Weight Watchers camp.

WOMAN #2. *(reading)* Church Parking Lot.

MAN #1. *(reading)* My Babysitter's House.

WOMAN #1. *(reading)* Dude Ranch.

MAN #2. *(reading)* Bathhouse.

WOMAN #2. *(reading)* Summer stock.

MAN #1. *(reading)* At Six Flags.

WOMAN #1. *(reading)* A woman's shoe store.

MAN #2. *(reading)* In the butt.*

WOMAN #2. *(reading)* My creaky bed.

MAN #1. *(reading)* YMCA.

WOMAN #1. *(reading)* My physician's office.

MAN #2. *(reading)* Honeymoon.

WOMAN #2. *(reading)* Under the boardwalk.

> *SLIDE #36:*
>
> Story #25176
>
> Where It Happened:
>
> Airplane

> *(**MAN #1** steps downstage)*

MAN #1. *(with childlike enthusiasm)* I was coming back to Boston from Florida and had to stop in Atlanta to board another plane. All of the seats in the waiting area were taken except for the one next to me. I was watching TV when this gorgeous girl came over and asked if she could sit down. She had blond hair, was about 5'7, had a slight southern accent and was a student at Tufts. *(He gives a "High-Five" to a male audience member in the front row.)* She asked me where I was sitting on the plane and said she was sitting about ten rows in back of me. She asked me if I wanted to sit next to her. I said sure. She asked me if I had a girlfriend. I said no. I asked her if she had a boyfriend. She said no. We boarded the plane and I told *my mom* I was moving seats! I walked back to where Julie was sitting. She let me take the window seat! After about 10 minutes she put her head on my shoulder and closed her eyes. I leaned forward and kissed her. We made out for about two minutes and she then pulled away. She whispered in my ear that she would be in the bathroom farthest back and that I should knock twice. About two minutes later I got up and walked back to the bathroom. I knocked on the door the way

* This line can be used as a "plant" line to encourage laughter.

she told me to. She opened the door. I quickly walked in and closed it behind me. She backed away and took off her shirt. She had on a bra but that came off too. I kissed her again. I then backed up and pulled down her sweat pants. I asked her to sit on the sink. I asked her if she wanted to continue and she said yes.

(He "High-Fives" the same audience member again.)

SLIDE #36 FADES TO BLACK.

*(*MAN #1 *sits.)*

MAN #2. I slowly undressed her as one would unwrap a fragile birthday present.

MAN #1. In front of me stood the first naked girl I had ever seen.

WOMAN #1. I'd never seen a nude man before and the sight is something I'll never forget. I thought his body was the most beautiful thing I'd ever seen. The muscles, the hair on his thighs even a couple of scars on his shoulder and forearm. It literally took my breath away.

MAN #2. There were stripes all over her skin from wearing different bathing suits. She looked like a bowl of mixed ice cream: strawberry in one place, vanilla in another, and chocolate here and there.

WOMAN #2. He was nude when he joined me on the bed. I touched his chest, and turned my hand so I could feel his beard on the softer skin on the top, and he kissed me.

WOMAN #1. He looked like a little Greek statue.

MAN #1. She was wearing a black bra that concealed nothing, and a black garter belt that supported black nylons. Her state was beyond nakedness.

MAN #2. She had large nipples and they were standing up hard. I thought, "Thank God for hotel air conditioning.

WOMAN #2. I had never seen a naked boy with a boner before.

MAN #1. I was stiff as Al Gore.

WOMAN #1. I wanted it so much, but it seemed too big.

MAN #2. 8 inches.

MAN #1. 9 inches.

WOMAN #2. 3 inches.

WOMAN #1. He let me put a condom on him and he detonated too soon, like they all do the first time. There's a reason condoms are sold three to a box.

WOMAN #2. I found myself standing in front of his door at the other end of the hall. I was naked in the moonlight at the top of the stairs, my T-shirt on the floor in my doorway. Suddenly, self-consciously, I quickly entered and clicked the door shut behind me. It was pitch black and cool. I fumbled for the edge of the bed and slid in, instantly feeling the heat of Curt's skin next to me. He was naked, with his back to me. I reached over to touch his back. He rolled over.

MAN #1. This is the first time I had ever seen a woman's body in the flesh. I stood there motionless, gaping, making no sign of intention to act for nearly a minute.

WOMAN #1. He looked like a little puppy waiting to get a treat.

MAN #2. She said…

WOMAN #2. I want to spend the night with you.

MAN #1. I want my first time to be your first time.

WOMAN #1. I want to give myself to you for your birthday.

MAN #2. Fuck, I can't find the words to say what I feel.

WOMAN #1. Shut off the lights.

MAN #1. But I want to look at you.

WOMAN #2. It undoes at the front.

MAN #2. Whoa. Those are real!

WOMAN #1. So you like my feet, huh?

WOMAN #2. Are you scared?

MAN #1. I'll stop if it hurts.

WOMAN #1. It's only me, silly.

MAN #2. I want this to be great for you.

MAN #1. Sue?

WOMAN #2. Mark?

MAN #1 & WOMAN #2. Do you wanna...

MAN #1. Sorry.

WOMAN #2. You first.

MAN #1 & WOMAN #2. Do you wanna make love with me?

MAN #2 & WOMAN #1. Yes.

MAN #1. Are you sure?

WOMAN #1. Yes.

MAN #2. Definitely.

WOMAN #2. I don't know.

MAN #1. Sure.

WOMAN #1. Ok.

MAN #2. Yep.

WOMAN #2. I don't know.

MAN #1. Yes.

WOMAN #1. Yes.

MAN #2. Yes.

WOMAN #2. I don't know.

MAN #1. Yes.

WOMAN #1. Yes.

MAN #2. Yes.

(*All look at* **WOMAN #2**.)

WOMAN #2. I caved in. Submitted to an ultimatum from 16-year-old Doug.

MAN #2. My brain said no, but my dick said yes...and guess who won.

WOMAN #1. It was all a game to them: territory lost, territory gained, and I played into it like a starving puppy dog.

MAN #1. Where I came from a girl didn't even want sex. It was just a bargaining tool on the table of long term relationships.

MAN #2. Anytime I tugged at her waist band, she would moan a whispered...

WOMAN #2. Noooo.

MAN #1. No didn't mean no in those days.

MAN #2. Do you like this, Jenny?

WOMAN #2. Mark, please don't, it's late.

MAN #1. And it doesn't always mean no today.

MAN #2. Do you trust me, Jenny?

WOMAN #2. Please Mark...stop!

> *SLIDE #37:*
>
> Story #3564
>
> Where It Happened:
>
> Harley Bar

Scene IV

(MAN #1 steps downstage and stares down the audience.)

MAN #1. I love to seduce women – the more forbidden, the better. Your girlfriend? Your wife? It's a challenge I can't resist. I was 24 and was running a biker bar and she was hanging out with Scott, one of my regulars. He'd been bitching that she wouldn't come across with the goodies and he was getting horny as hell.

(MAN #2 steps downstage and stands next to MAN #1.)

SLIDE #38:

Story #417

Where It Happened:

Motel

MAN #2. Jenny went to school in another town and had noticed me first as I had edged her out in the Minnesota State Scholarship exams in the seventh grade. We spent almost every waking moment of that summer together. It was a platonic friendship at first. Then at the eighth grade Thanksgiving sock hop, Jenny put the moves on me. For the next three years it was kissing and rubbing hands above the waist. She wouldn't go further because she wanted to get married in white.

SLIDE #38 FADES TO BLACK.

MAN #1. When Scott brought her into the joint for the first time, I was at the bar. Kerrie was wearing one of those short little sundresses and showing a lot of leg. The cleavage I saw when she sat at the bar showed she had a first class body, too. I poured a drink for Scott and carded her. She was 18. I poured her a Coke and poured myself a strong shot of 151 rum. As we talked, I took a sip and "spilled" most of it in her glass. With a wink, I left the bar and went back to my office.

MAN #2. I wasn't popular in school; I dated no one, but Jenny went on dates. I burned with jealousy, but there was nothing I could do. Jenny's parents were always pressuring her to date the Bishop's son. Meanwhile, I was getting more and more discouragement from Jenny's parents. They made it clear that I was not to get serious about Jenny. Jenny went to her prom with the Bishop's son. I was too heartbroken to go to mine with anybody but Jenny, but her parents had put their foot down...firmly on me.

MAN #1. A few minutes later, I heard a ruckus and ran out to find this other chick trying to beat the hell out of Kerrie. This girl had ripped the top strap of Kerrie's dress and was trying to yank it off. I got a great view of Kerrie's bikini panties before I stopped the fight. Kerrie was frightened and a little banged up. I walked her back to my office and told her to lie down on the couch until she caught her breath. She was clearly upset and a little frightened about going back to the bar. I rolled a doobie and lit up. Walking over to the couch, I offered it to her. She had never smoked and it took some coaching to teach her how to inhale and hold it for a minute. With the 151 and the smoke, she was flying high.

MAN #2. Jenny was on my doorstep at 6 AM the morning after the prom. This prince of Jenny's parents' dreams had driven Jenny to a seedy motel. When Jenny refused to get out of the car, he raped her right on the front seat, pushed her out of the car and drove off.

MAN #1. I leaned over and kissed her forehead, her cheek, then covered her mouth with my lips as I moved my hand up to her gorgeous breasts. She was startled at first and grabbed my hand to move it away. I moved my hand down to the hem of her dress and started lifting it slowly toward the promised land. I heard little noises coming from her. She was saying, "No, no, no" very quietly, almost under her breath. I reached that short band of material that holds a woman's panties on, that piece at the side that's not even an inch wide. Her virginal white bikinis were about to drop to the floor like a white flag of surrender. She grabbed my hand again, her last effort to stop my onslaught. I stood up and stripped to claim my prize.

MAN #2. Jenny was covered with marks and bruises. There were teeth marks and punch bruises all over her body.

MAN #1. Her dress was bunched around her waist and her bra was loose…her legs were wide apart, giving me complete access to her pussy.

MAN #2. Jenny called her parents, but their only concern was that she had spoiled her biggest and best marriage prospect by behaving so badly. The idea of date rape was far from ever thought of in those days. Jenny was accused of having led him on by being at such a seedy motel, and besides, it was ok because they were soon to be married anyway. Her family sent her to Salt Lake City. I never saw or heard from Jenny again. And none of her friends heard from her.

MAN #1. She definitely enjoyed her first time.

    *(***MAN #1** *sits.* **MAN #2** *sits.)*

WOMAN #2. I was drunk.

WOMAN #1. I got drunk.

MAN #2. Drunk and stoned.

MAN #1. I can't recall how much Jack Daniel's I had but it was a lot.

WOMAN #1. We sat around doing shots, a little XTC…

WOMAN #2. I was so drunk it was hilarious!

MAN #2. We were wasted.

MAN #1. Smashed.

WOMAN #2. Passed out.

WOMAN #1. Cocked off my ass.

MAN #2. Baked as fuck.

MAN #1. I threw up all over her.

WOMAN #2. Oh my God, what am I doing?

    SLIDE #39:

    Story #6985

    Where It Happened:

    N/A

WOMAN #1. I am not going to give any details on where it happened or anything to reveal my identity. I am just going to say I lost my virginity to one of those assholes who makes a game of seducing innocent girls and bragging about his conquests afterward. So listen, asshole...

(**WOMAN #1** *steps downstage.*)

I might be that girl you seduced the other night, taking advantage of her innocence and naivete. And if I am that girl and you are that guy, I am going to see to it that you regret it. Because I have made careful notes on all that happened and I have the names of three guys that you bragged to, and other corroborating evidence. You pride yourself on how clever you are and how well you succeed in everything you attempt. And you look forward to a successful career, in business and then in politics. Well, I want you to know that the minute you achieve your first big success – a prestigious appointment, election to an important office, or whatever, I am going to come forward and tell all, and let's see how you weasel out of this. So, you might be Danny up in Montana or Fred in Maine or someone else, somewhere else. But your little game of deflowering innocent, trusting girls is going to come back on you. You son of a bitch.

(*blackout*)

SLIDE #40:

Only 1 out of every 3 girls who lose their virginity before the age of 18 claim their experience was "wanted."

SLIDE #41: [AUTO]

90% of acquaintance rapes involve alcohol.

SLIDE #42: [AUTO]

_____% (*insert number from audience survey*) of the females in this audience felt pressured into having sex.

(**WOMAN #2** *sits in blackout.*)

Scene V

SLIDE #43: [AUTO]

Story #8115

Where It Happened:

Basement Floor

(lights up after slide)

(MAN #2 is already seated centerstage, on the lip of the stage.)

MAN #2. She was a friend of my cousin's who was always around the house. My age, wavy blond, shoulder-length hair, blue eyes and a smile so sweet it made you cringe not to kiss her when she flashed it. One night when she had stayed a little too late watching a scary movie I was nominated by my aunt to walk the poor dear home. I was more than happy to do it. Perhaps I could tell her my feelings about her. Perhaps she felt the same way. Perhaps I might even get a kiss out of the deal. As we neared her house she complained of being chilly. What was a poor young gentleman to do but put his arm around the maiden-in-distress? It came out that my cousin mentioned to Lisa that I liked her. I gallantly confessed that I found almost nothing about her I did not like. She tilted her head onto my shoulder and gave me a sweet thank you nudge. I didn't get a kiss goodnight. Just a thank you and a phone number. She told me to call her when I got home.

(WOMAN #2 and MAN #1 step downstage, and turn slightly, looking away from each other.)

MAN #1. Won't I wake your parents?

WOMAN #2. Nah, I live with my dad and he's been in bed since 8:00. He wouldn't wake if the house caved in.

MAN #2. I sprinted all the way home. We talked until dawn and still had more to say when her dad poked his head in her bedroom door and told her to…

WOMAN #1. Get the hell off the phone.

MAN #2. She said she would come over after school. I fell

asleep with a ten foot wide grin. We were kind of awkward together that afternoon. It's one thing to spill out your heart and soul over the phone in the middle of the night, but it's totally different when you gotta face the person the next day. We watched a movie in silence. Lisa asked for a blanket, complaining of being chilly again, and then offered to share half of it. Lisa's foot began to move slowly up my leg beneath the cover as my hand began to wander up her leg. The movie ended around eleven and this time I volunteered to walk her home. Our arms went around each other immediately and soon we arrived at her house.

WOMAN #2. Can you walk me to my door?

MAN #1. Sure.

MAN #2. This time I did get a goodnight kiss. We kissed standing in her back porch for twenty minutes. Then we kind of fell into a near-by chair. Our hands wandered in and out of each other's shirts and all over everywhere else. When we finally came up for air it was almost 1:00 AM.

MAN #1. Should I phone you when I get home?

WOMAN #2. I gotta get some sleep or I'll pass out in school.

MAN #1. Do you wanna be my girlfriend?

WOMAN #2. You mean go out with you? Officially?

MAN #1. Yeah.

WOMAN #2. Of course...

MAN #2. I kissed her again. It was another fifteen minutes before I finally tore myself away and floated home five feet off the ground. I couldn't wait to see her and kiss her and hold her. I was crazy about it. I was crazy about her being crazy about me. She came over that evening again and we "watched a movie" under a blanket with my cousin on the other end of the sectional pretending she didn't notice us carrying on like two long lost lovers. Kissing and fondling and whispering in each other's ear. I felt her up that night too. Then my Aunt came into the room and, with a glance at our flushed faces and tousled hair, suggested that it was...

WOMAN #1. Getting kinda late.

MAN #2. Off we went on the short little trek to her father's home. We walked slowly, dizzy and feeling mushy in the head. Holding on to one another like it was our last day alive. When we got to her back porch we wasted no time falling into the old chair. After 1:00 AM, she suggested we go for a walk to cool down. Soon we arrived in front of my Aunt's house again.

MAN #1. Do you wanna go in the house?

WOMAN #2. You could sneak me in?

MAN #1. We'd have to go into the basement, they'd hear us anywhere else...

MAN #2. We went around to the back door. We crept through the kitchen and down into the basement. I flicked on the light and smelled the musky, moldy, laundry detergent smell you smell in all basements. It wasn't the most romantic place but we were beyond caring. There was no longer any point in pretending we didn't know what was going to happen. Perhaps I was biased but I couldn't think of a girl I had ever met who was more beautiful than her right then. I looked around for some place to lay her down. The only feasible location was a pile of laundry in front of the furnace. So there we went, trembling and grinning with the excitement only known by two people about to have sex for the first time.

(lights fade to half.)

WOMAN #2. Do you have a condom?

MAN #1. I think I'm falling in love with you.

WOMAN #2. Me too.

(Lights up on **WOMAN #1**.*)*

WOMAN #1. I don't want to make a confession. I just want to let everyone know how hot I am from some of these stories.

(Blackout as...)

SLIDE #43 FADES TO BLACK.

WOMAN #2. You know, with the lights out, completely dark, you can really use your imagination. It's kind of neat. You can pretend anything...

Scene VI

(In black.)

MAN #1. Relax.

WOMAN #1. Are you ready?

MAN #2. I can't believe we're doing this.

WOMAN #2. What are you waiting for?

MAN #1. Holy crap.

WOMAN #1. This is kind of weird.

MAN #2. Where is it?

WOMAN #2. Is it in?

MAN #1. Get on the bed.

WOMAN #1. You can go lower.

MAN #2. Can I put it in without the condom?

WOMAN #2. Damn, I'm flexible.

MAN #1. Oops.

WOMAN #1. Please you can go lower.

MAN #2. That's never happened before.

WOMAN #2. You're hurting me.

MAN #1. Should I stop?

WOMAN #1. Go lower.

MAN #2. You want it.

WOMAN #2. Yes.

MAN #1. No.

WOMAN #1. Go slow.

WOMAN #2. I'm embarrassed…I need your help.

MAN #1. This is it.

WOMAN #1. This is it.

MAN #2. This is it.

*(lights up soft on **WOMAN #2** only.)*

WOMAN #2. Looking back on it, I should have closed my legs right then and there. But I was in love.

(lights fade to black.)

MAN #1. Oh yes!

WOMAN #1. Yeah, just like that!

MAN #2. Ohhhhhhhhhhhhhhhhhhhh…

WOMAN #2. Yes!

MAN #1. Yes!

WOMAN #1. Don't stop.

MAN #2. There goes my V-card!

MAN #1. Oh my God, I'm having sex!

WOMAN #1. Oh God.

MAN #2. Oh Jesus.

WOMAN #2. Oh God.

MAN #1. Oh God.

MAN #1, MAN #2, WOMAN #1 & WOMAN #2. Oh God.

(*lights bump up to full!*)

SLIDE #44:

Story #1382

Where It Happened:

It will happen on my wedding night!

Scene VII

(MAN #1 is downstage center holding a small Bible..)

MAN #1. Sex is a gift from God that is given to men and women to be enjoyed within a loving and committed marriage. I am waiting until marriage because I am a born again, Bible-believing Christian who understands the dimensions of sex. When I give myself for the first time to my wife, I will be giving her a piece of my humanity and will become one flesh with her. All of these people that had sex with people who were not their husband or wife have settled for second best and may suffer emotional, spiritual, or physical ruin.

SLIDE #45:

Story #34

MAN #1. The body is not for sexual sin but for God.

SLIDE #47:

Story #345

MAN #1. No fornicator shall enter the kingdom of heaven.

SLIDE #49:

Story #20705

MAN #1. You will be damned if you do this.

SLIDE #51:

Story #926

MAN #1. Lust and fornication is wrong.

SLIDE #53:

Story #345

MAN #1. You are going to hell, unless you repent of your sins.

SLIDE #55:

Story #21525

MAN #1. Amen and Amen.

SLIDE #57:

Story #944

MAN #1. Praise Jesus.

SLIDE #59:

Story #926

MAN #1. Oh yes, sex is appealing, but its ultimate reward when done through lust is shameful deviance, unhappiness, anger, disrespect for others, laziness, a "mush-brain" mentality, and most sadly and importantly, a complete disregard for God. Especially reviling is this site's whole purpose of existence. A shrine to the loss of sexual pureness. One more watermark for the steady degradation of a person wrapped in sin. By the grace of God over sin and flesh, I will never return to this site again!

SLIDE #59 FADES.

(MAN #1 *starts to walk toward his seat and then turns back to the audience.*)

SLIDE #60:

Story #717

MAN #1 *(cont.)* You guys need Jesus.

(blackout)

SLIDE #60 FADES TO BLACK.

(MAN #1 *sits in blackout*)

Scene VIII

MAN #2. Jesus.

WOMAN #1. Oh God.

MAN #2. God.

WOMAN #2. Jesus.

MAN #1. Oh God.

WOMAN #1. God.

MAN #2. Jesus.

WOMAN #2. Oh God.

(*Lights come up soft on* MAN #1 *only,*)

MAN #1. I thought my parents must have heard the bed springs, because we were making a ton of noise.

(*Lights come up soft on* WOMAN #1 *only.*)

WOMAN #1. I was tossing my head around trying to get enough air to breathe, and my whole world was beginning to spin.

(*Lights come up soft on* MAN #2 *only.*)

MAN #2. Here I am, as virgin as virgin gets, making love to the most beautiful girl I have ever seen.

(*Lights come up soft on* WOMAN #2 *only.*)

WOMAN #2. It felt…like lightning.

(*Lights go out*)

MAN #1. Oh my God, I'm fucking Teri!

WOMAN #1. Oh yes, give it to me, College Boy!

MAN #2. My name is Tom.

WOMAN #2. Ouch!

MAN #1. Oh my God, I'm fucking Teri!

WOMAN #1. This isn't working.

MAN #2. It's almost over.

WOMAN #2. Now, now, now!

(*Lights come up on* MAN #1.)

MAN #1. I couldn't. It was too much, and I was just too scared. I told her I couldn't.

(Lights fade out)

WOMAN #1. Do it, damn it!

MAN #2. Oh boy!

WOMAN #2. I screamed.

MAN #1. I cried out.

WOMAN #1. I bit him.

MAN #2. I grabbed her long red hair.

WOMAN #2. I wrapped my legs around him.

MAN #1. This is it!

WOMAN #1. This is it!

MAN #2. Wait!

WOMAN #2. What?

MAN #1. I've got to pull out!

(lights up as...)

SLIDE #61:

Story #1436

Where It Happened:

Make-out Central

*(**WOMAN #1** is downstage.)*

WOMAN #1. The year was 1966. It was the summer before 9th grade when a family from California moved into my neighborhood. The boy was named Dennis and was so knock-down cute that I could have died. I wouldn't have had a chance with him since he was going to be a senior, but he had a sister named Karen who was going to be in my grade. Karen and her brother had a deal that he would double date with her and she would fix him up. On the very first date we went to make-out central. If I wanted to stay in the picture I knew what I had to do. Blankets, Kleenex and Coke were provided. It was explained that you wouldn't get pregnant if you douched with the Coke afterwards. I didn't know how so I got a demonstration by Karen who lay down and screwed her boyfriend right in front of her brother and me and then showed how to do the Coke. When it came to my turn, I was so nervous with the other two watching me I just couldn't do it. Finally Karen and her date held my legs while...the pain was beyond words but I simply bit my lip. Dennis asked if I was a virgin but I wanted to be cool so I said I wasn't. All he could say was, "Damn, she's tight." I said that I hadn't ever done it with someone so big before. Then the two boys held me in a squatting position and Karen shook up the Coke and jammed it in me. The fizzing Coke stung like hell and everybody made fun of me. It was what was expected if I was to gorge myself at Mr. Steak and Dairy Queen and be seen hanging around with Dennis. It was open wide, let the drilling happen, rinse now, and be glad there's no pain. That's why I called him Dennis the Dentist. The Coke-douche was so gross. No matter how well you wiped, the insides of your legs were always sticky from the sugar afterward. When they would have second helpings, the boys asked us to open our legs especially wide because they didn't like the stickiness anymore than we did. We always parked in the last row at the drive-in movies so us girls could jump out and douche in the weeds behind the car. The worst thing about the Coke douches? They don't work. Abortions weren't legal, but my father got me one anyway. It cost $1500 and when I got my driver's licence later my father told me I could have gotten a car but the money went someplace else instead...a 1968 Fiat 500 cost $1465.

(blackout)

*(***WOMAN #2*** sits.)*

SLIDE #61 FADES TO BLACK.

SLIDE #62: [AUTO]

_____ % *(insert number from audience survey)* of this audience did not use a contraceptive for their first time.

SLIDE #62 FADES TO BLACK.

MAN #2. I think I'm going to…

WOMAN #2. Don't stop!

MAN #1. I can't stop!

WOMAN #1. Sparks went through my entire body.

WOMAN #2. My breasts caught on fire.

MAN #1. My toes went numb!

WOMAN #1. My legs started to shake.

MAN #2. My balls felt like they were going to burst!

WOMAN #1. My nipples got all tingley!

MAN #2. I couldn't hold it any longer!

MAN #1. Yes!

WOMAN #1. Yes!

MAN #2. No!

WOMAN #2. Now!

MAN #1. Oh boy!

WOMAN #1. Holy shit!

MAN #2. Here I go!

WOMAN #2. We're having sex!

(*A few flashes of a strobe light.*)

MAN #1. *(ad libbing)* OH! Yes! Now! Please!

WOMAN #1. *(ad libbing)* OH! Yes! Now! Please!

MAN #2. *(ad libbing)* OH! Yes! Now! Please! Choo-Choo!

WOMAN #2. *(ad libbing)* OH! Yes! Now! Please!

(**WOMAN #2** *crosses downstage.* **WOMAN #1** *screams.*)

(*Strobes stop.*)

WOMAN #2. I screamed it hurt so much.

(*lights fade up*)

SLIDE #63:
Story #7188

Where It Happened:

At Home

WOMAN #2. I felt as if I were being ripped apart, and tears began streaming down my cheeks. Jeff tried to comfort me, holding me to him, kissing away my tears, and saying sweet things. After a minute or two, the pain started to subside, and I told him so, just so he wouldn't feel so guilty. He pulled out a little, and pushed back in, but it instantly brought back the pain, so I begged him to remain still a little longer. After a little bit, he began moving, and this time, the pain, was more bearable. He continued moving in me, and it began to feel very good. I didn't understand what was happening, but there was something unfolding within me that I couldn't stop. I started moaning and gasping, my breath coming in hard, short breaths. By then, I was meeting each of his thrusts, which were coming harder and faster. Each time I met his thrust, I felt as if I were going to explode. I didn't know what was happening at all, only that it was spreading throughout my body. I began shaking my head on the pillow, and before I knew it, I screamed. After, we just laid there, holding each other...

SLIDE #63 FADES TO BLACK.

(**WOMAN #2** *sits.*)

Scene IX

MAN #1. She could have asked for anything I possessed in those moments.

WOMAN #1. I began to cry and he took me in his arms and held me close.

MAN #2. The feeling I had at that moment is something I hope I will always carry with me.

MAN #1. We lay there for about 10 seconds.

(long beat)

WOMAN #2. I love you, Kyle.

WOMAN #1. He kissed me gently and asked if I came. I didn't know what to say, so I lied and said yes.

MAN #2. A thirty second commercial lasts longer than I did.

MAN #1. I love you too.

WOMAN #1. I was relieved it didn't last too long. The sooner it was over, the less time to get a bellyful of baby.

MAN #2. As I recall, I was pretty good at it.

WOMAN #2. I didn't sleep for days until I got my period.

MAN #1. She asked if this meant if we were going out.

WOMAN #1. It was the best I have ever felt in my life.

MAN #2. It was the most passionate thing of my entire life.

MAN #1. It was mind blowing.

WOMAN #2. It was horrible. He had no idea how to get a scared to death girl ready and it went rather quickly. We used a condom, and Midnight Starr played over and over in the jam box. I hate that group to this day! It hurt so bad...and all I could keep thinking was, "He has his socks on!" I expected so much more! To this day when I think of losing my virginity, I still think, "But he didn't take off his socks."

MAN #2. It was kind of like turning 16, 18, or 21. You think you're going to wake up and everything is going to be different or better somehow, but it isn't. You're just another year older with a license, pack of smokes, or beer.

WOMAN #1. It was like Christmas morning...only worse.

MAN #1. In 1984, my Aunt got a flu shot, caught the flu and died in her bed. The whole family raised its collective eyebrow when she left me her house, her meager savings and her insurance proceeds, naming me in her will as the man who made her "whole." I played dumb of course, but everyone suspected what they had never suspected before. Fuck 'em.

MAN #2. She left for college a week later and never came back.

WOMAN #2. Love is a contact sport and if you can't stand an occasional bruise, then get off the field.

WOMAN #1. I learned that no one can love two people. His wife deserves his full attention and I stole that from her. I didn't think it was too important at first but as we became closer I could see him suffer from the lies he was telling himself and his family. I hope he knows what he means to me and what he meant to me that wondrous Friday night. I hope he really felt the things he said he felt. And I hope he finds those things with his wife.

MAN #1. She gave me a pair of panties as a remembrance. I keep them in my file cabinet to this day. I haven't looked at them for years and I think it's time to do so.

WOMAN #2. He gave me crabs.

WOMAN #1. I still have the Metallica shirt he wore that night.

MAN #1. I still have her picture in my wallet.

MAN #2. I still truly love her and hardly a day goes by that I don't think of her, more than 30 years since I last saw her. I would leave my wife of 28 years if Linda would only ask me.

MAN #1. I would love to see her again.

WOMAN #2. I don't know where he is now.

MAN #1. I miss her.

WOMAN #1. I miss you.

MAN #2. I proposed.

WOMAN #1. Today he is my husband and still the only lover I've had.

MAN #1. This morning was the 35th anniversary of my First Time. I celebrated by bringing my wife a cup of coffee an hour before the alarm was set to go off.

MAN #2. I love him…and I want to marry him.

WOMAN #2. Call me a slut if you like, but I am learning with each one and I know what I want in a husband now. Best of all, this has been my favorite course of study in college and I'm thinking of going to grad school to pursue this undeclared major.

MAN #1. Would a girl ever want me? Was I attractive? Was I desirable? Lisa had answered all these questions in one night, and I still had as much respect for her as I ever had. She had done what she wanted, because she wanted to do it and for no other reason. She had nothing to prove, nothing to gain, she wasn't using sex for some ulterior motive. She just did it cause she wanted me. And that made me feel pretty damn good.

WOMAN #1. My first time was incredible. Therefore, I'm not going to ruin the memory by sharing it with people I don't even know.

WOMAN #2. The moral of the story is…don't fuck your friends.

MAN #2. That hour will live long in my heart and hers as well, I'm sure…

(**MAN #2** *steps downstage.*)

…So this submission is dedicated to Megan.

(**MAN #1** *steps downstage.*)

MAN #1. I want to dedicate this story to my ever-faithful first, Maria.

(**WOMAN #1** *steps downstage.*)

WOMAN #1. Shag, if you ever read this, remember Debbie thinks about you every day.

(**WOMAN #2** *steps downstage.*)

WOMAN #2. Merci pour tout, Patrick.

MAN #2. Bueno gracias.

MAN #1. Ciao.

(The cast prep cards.)

SLIDE #64:

Story #35357

WOMAN #1. Thanks, Josh, for showing me that there is more to life out there. You are my soul mate, and my inspiration. I love you with all my heart!

SLIDE #65:

Story #33474

MAN #1. Jen, you mean the world to me. We will be together forever.

SLIDE #66:

Story #26253

WOMAN #2. Tyler, thank you for helping with my first experience. You are my bestest friend and always will be.

SLIDE #67:

Story #2263

MAN #2. Amanda, if you read this give me a call because Nolan wants to do it again...or if any women out there are interested in having sex, give me a call.

SLIDE #68:

_____ % *(insert number from audience survey)* of this Audience still keeps in touch with their First Time partner.)

(cast reads actual audience comments from the cards.)

MAN #1. *(reading)* You have a small penis and moobs (man boobs)!

WOMAN #1. *(reading)* He's married to my best friend now. It's cool though - he looks like Screech from Saved by the Bell.

MAN #2. *(reading)* Thanks after growing up fundamentalist, I really needed that!

WOMAN #2. *(reading)* I'm sorry I made you think I was 'preggers' that April Fool's Day.

MAN #1. *(reading)* Size does matter, not just the motion of the ocean, cause it takes a hell of a long time to get to England in a row boat.

WOMAN #1. *(reading)* It took my longer to fill out this card than it did to lose my virginity.

MAN #2. *(reading)* I'm glad I don't have to see you anymore and no, I will not explain why we are broke up again. Also, you're not as attractive as I remember.

WOMAN #2. *(reading)* Please stop calling me. I don't want to be with you again. I'll call INS!

MAN #1. *(reading)* My therapist would like to have a word with you.

WOMAN #1. *(reading)* You better start paying your rent or I am gonna start selling your cats.

MAN #2. *(reading)* I wish it was bigger. Like your cousin's!

WOMAN #2. *(reading)* Give me back the money you owe me from the loan I cosigned for you!

MAN #1. *(reading)* By the way, after we had sex, I realized that, yeah, I was gay.

WOMAN #1. *(reading)* Where are my Depeche Mode CD's?

MAN #2. *(reading)* Sorry I was wearing leopard print granny underwear!

WOMAN #2. I love you…

(cast continues to read audience member names, the same from the beginning of the show, in the same order.)

MAN #1. *(reading)* Julie.

WOMAN #1. *(reading)* Joseph.

MAN #2. *(reading)* Erin.

WOMAN #2. *(reading)* Eric.

MAN #1. *(reading)* Ashley.

WOMAN #1. *(reading)* Asshole.

MAN #2. *(reading)* Carol.

WOMAN #2. *(reading)* Robbie.

MAN #1. *(reading)* Don't remember.

WOMAN #1. *(reading)* Fred.

MAN #2. *(reading)* Andrea.

WOMAN #2. *(reading)* Christopher.

MAN #1. *(reading)* Linda.

WOMAN #1. *(reading)* Dwayne.

MAN #2. *(reading)* Linda.

WOMAN #2. *(reading)* Joey.

SLIDE #68 FADES TO BLACK.

(Actors take a moment, lower their cards, and say the <u>name of their actual first time partners</u>.)

MAN #1. NAME.

WOMAN #1. NAME.

MAN #2. NAME.

WOMAN #2. NAME.

WOMAN #1. I'll never forget that first time.

MAN #1. Nothing compared to that first time.

MAN #2. I will always remember my first time.

WOMAN #2. I will never forget it.

MAN #1. I will never forget it.

WOMAN #1. It hurt like hell.

MAN #2. I will never forget it.

WOMAN #2. But he didn't take off his socks!

(All turn upstage and walk back towards their stools and then look up, backs to the audience, to face the screen.)

SLIDE #69:

Story #41022

SLIDE #70:

I just wanted to say that I think it's great that there's a website devoted to first times.

SLIDE #71: [AUTO]

Maybe everyone will realize that this one "brief" experience doesn't have to be such a huge life changing moment.

SLIDE #72: [AUTO]

Why do we expect so much from it? A first time is just that...a first time.

SLIDE #73: [AUTO]

And like other firsts, your first step, your first word...it's rarely your best. It's just a first.

SLIDE #74: [AUTO]

So thanks for putting up this website. Maybe now we can all concentrate on what's really important...

SLIDE #75: [AUTO]

The next time.

SLIDE #76: [AUTO]

Because it gets a whole lot better.

TYPED ON LETTER BY LETTER

SLIDE #76 FADES TO BLACK (AUTO).

(The final song used in the Preshow plays as...)

SLIDE #77: [AUTO]

MY FIRST TIME

(Actors bow and exit.)

SLIDE #79:

After seeing this show, 100% of this audience will want to have sex tonight.

SLIDE #80: [AUTO]

Those who can't find a partner will turn to the internet.

(house lights up.)

SLIDE #81: [AUTO]

MY FIRST TIME *(logo)*

www.MyFirstTimeThePlay.com

My First Time proudly supports www.Scarleteen. com, the independent, comprehensive and inclusive sexuality education site for young adults, which has served up progressive sex ed for millions internationally since 1998.

The End

From the Reviews of
MY FIRST TIME...

"Funny and touching to sweet, sexy and silly!"
- *The Village Voice*

"One of New York's best new plays! Phenomenal!"
- EdgeNewYork.com

"One of the most entertaining plays I've seen this year."
- CurtainUp.com

"A diverting evening of first-time tales that is by turns comical, erotic, sentimental, galling, heart-rendering, and even mildly political."
- TheGlobeandMail.com

"A terrific choice for date night!"
- BroadwayWorld.com

"Davenport takes a sensational topic and turns it into an instrument by which he reminds everyone in the room that their similarities greatly outnumber their differences."
- MonstersandCritics.com

"Hilarious!" - DailyCandy.com

''The theatrical equivalent of a date movie...80 minutes of titillation!" - Newsday.com

"Provocative, amusing and moving!" - *The New York Post*

OTHER TITLES AVAILABLE FROM SAMUEL FRENCH

ADRIFT IN MACAO
Book and Lyrics by Christopher Durang
Music by Peter Melnick

Full Length / Musical / 4m, 3f / Unit Sets

Set in 1952 in Macao, China, *Adrift In Macao* is a loving parody of film noir movies. Everyone that comes to Macao is waiting for something, and though none of them know exactly what that is, they hang around to find out. The characters include your film noir standards, like Laureena, the curvacious blonde, who luckily bumps into Rick Shaw, the cynical surf and turf casino owner her first night in town. She ends up getting a job singing in his night club – perhaps for no reason other than the fact that she looks great in a slinky dress. And don't forget about Mitch, the American who has just been framed for murder by the mysterious villain McGuffin. With songs and quips, puns and farcical shenanigans, this musical parody is bound to please audiences of all ages.

OTHER TITLES AVAILABLE FROM SAMUEL FRENCH

GUTENBERG! THE MUSICAL!
Scott Brown and Anthony King

2m / Musical Comedy

In this two-man musical spoof, a pair of aspiring playwrights perform a backers' audition for their new project - a big, splashy musical about printing press inventor Johann Gutenberg. With an unending supply of enthusiasm, Bud and Doug sing all the songs and play all the parts in their crass historical epic, with the hope that one of the producers in attendance will give them a Broadway contract – fulfilling their ill-advised dreams.

"A smashing success!"
- *The New York Times*

"Brilliantly realized and side-splitting!
- *New York Magazine*

"There are lots of genuine laughs in Gutenberg!"
- *New York Post*